For Andrew, a real firecracker—B. F.

For Matthew, a little sparkler—C. M.

Margaret K. McElderry Books

An imprint of Simon & Schuster Children's Publishing Division

1230 Avenue of the Americas, New York, New York 10020

Text copyright © 2007 by Betsy Franco

Illustrations copyright © 2007 by Charlotte Middleton

Book design by Debra Sfetsios

The text for this book is set in Diotima.

The illustrations for this book are rendered in mixed media, consisting of drawing, collage, and computer design.

Manufactured in Mexico

10 9 8 7 6 5 4 3 2 1

Library of Congress Cataloging-in-Publication Data

Franco, Betsy.

Summer beat / Betsy Franco ; illustrated by Charlotte Middleton.—1st ed.

p. cm.

Summary: Two friends celebrate the sounds and sights of summer.

ISBN-13: 978-1-4169-1237-8

ISBN-10: 1-4169-1237-1 (hardcover)

[1. Summer—Fiction. 2. Noise—Fiction. 3. Stories in rhyme.] I. Middleton, Charlotte, ill. II. Title.

PZ8.3.F84765Sum 2007

[E]—dc22

2005029546

Summer Beat

Betsy Franco

Illustrated by Charlotte Middleton

MARGARET K. McELDERRY BOOKS

New York London Toronto Sydney

Clackity-

clack,

clackity-

clack.

My skateboard on the sidewalk squares.

Gliding to Joe's,

clackity-

clack.

The sidewalk tune rings through the air.

Wuf,

wuf,

wooooof,

wuf,

wuf,

woooooof.

Rusty pretends he's standing guard.

"Hey, Joe."

"Hey, Em."

Rusty licks me

into the yard.

Shhh shhh,

shhh shhh.

Sprinkler spritzing

on the lawn.

Skip-
j
u
m
p
in!
Shhh shhh.

Water tingles,
cold and
strong.

Swish

    swoosh,   *swish*

         swoosh.

Hammock swings
between the
trees.

Rustle, rustle, rustle, rustle.

Leaves shuffle in the breeze.

Bizzle-bzzz,

bizzle-bzzz.

Bumblebee comes zipping by.

Bizzle-bzzz,

bizzle-bizzle.

Hold my breath and off it flies.

Pat

a   pat

tat   a

tat,   tat

tat.

Race for cover from the drizzle.

Raindrops stop,
    pat . . . .
        tat,

before the coals *fizzle fizzle.*

Juicy burgers

sssss sizzle.

Find a plate.

Grab a bun.

"Time for games!"

"Time for games!"

Everyone gathers on the street.

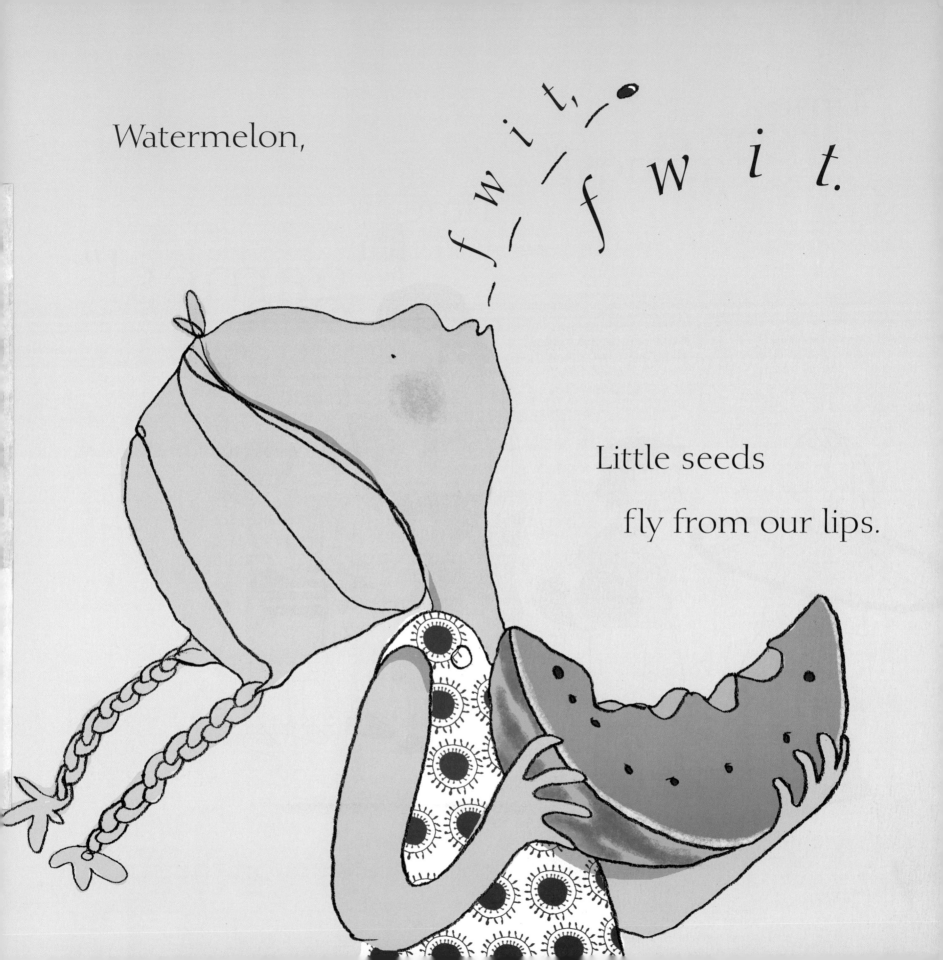

Watermelon,

f w i t, f w i t.

Little seeds
fly from our lips.

Chump,
chump
corn on the cob.

Crackle,

c
r
u
n
c
h

munchy

chips.

Licking fingers,

slup, *slup.*

Being messy's half the fun!

Tha-*thump,* *tha-*thump, tha-*tha-*thump. *thump,* thump.

A three-legged race.

We can't be beat!

Whoosh pumf, whoosh pumf

Tossing water balloons around.

I throw to Joe.

Pop!

Spltt!

Our yellow balloon
smacks the ground!

Zip

hissssss,

dız

hissssss.

Lighting sparklers

on a stick.

We wave our stars and dance around. Hisssssss-sss-s-s. They burn out quick.

Flappity-*flap,*

flappity-*flap.*

Fancy wheels—red, white, and blue.

We all parade

flappity-flap.

Down the block,

two by two.

Bam pop, bam pop.

Fireworks start for the Fourth of July!

Tzooooooooooooo

bang.

Tzooooooooooo

bang.

Climb the hill to watch the sky.

Zeeeeeeeeeeee bam bam.

Zeeeeeeeeeeeee

bam bam.

Colors burst as we lie back.

Fooooooooosh boom.

Fooooooooosh boom boom.

Over our heads,
poppity-crack!

Walking home to fading sounds.

Boom

boom

pop.

Boom

boom

pop.

Time for bed.

Trip, *trop.*

Climb
the
ladder
to
the
top.

Snuffle,

snort,

snuffle,

snort.

Treet- treet,

treet- treet.

Summer sounds never stop.